# Candles All Around

## A Chanukah Miracle Story

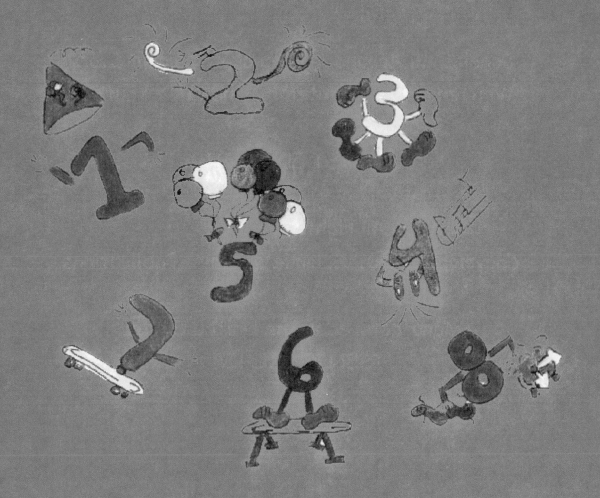

Written and Illustrated by Sharon R. Kaufman

Candles All Around: A Chanukah Miracle Story
Written and Illustrated by Sharon R. Kaufman

FIRST EDITION

Manufactured in the United States
ISBN 1449534589

Dedicated to all of my nieces and nephews.
May your lives be filled with many beautiful miracles.
I love you very much.

Aunt Sharon

It was the morning of the first night of Chanukah, and all the candles were snuggled next to one another in the order they were to be placed in the Menorah.

Out of nowhere, the candles jumped out of bed!

They could hear the happy sounds of children playing.

They could smell the latkes (potato pancakes) frying.

The candles began running and jumping around in excitement.

They had been waiting for this moment all year long.

Chanukah was finally here,
and they did not want to miss one minute!

But there was one candle that was not having a good time.

The Shamas candle was

very upset.

The Shamas has a very important job.

She brings light to all the other candles.

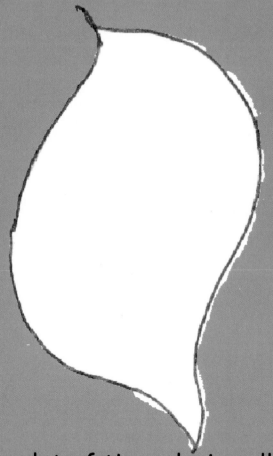

And she spent a lot of time placing all the candles in order from 1 to 8.

So the Shamas raised her voice above all the noise.

"Attention Chanukah candles," but no one listened.

She tried again, "Attention Chanukah candles." Still, the candles continued to play.

One last time, "Attention Chanukah candles."

But the candles were not listening.

They were having way too much fun!

Candle Number 1 was bouncing so high, she almost touched the sky.

Candle Number 2 pretended he was a cow...moo, moo.

Candle Number 3 was dancing

with glee.

Candle Number 4 was laughing on the floor.

Candle Number 5 wanted to take a drive.

Candle Number 6 was playing drums with some sticks.

Candle Number 7 was eating cookies straight from the oven.

And Candle Number 8 was rolling around in a crazy state.

Finally, the Shamas whistled so loudly that all the candles stopped right where they were.

The Sun was going to go down soon, and she needed to get everyone in order.

"That's more like it. We have a job to do. So let's all help each other get lined up."

The candles looked at each other, and began to cry. They did not know what to do.

"We need a miracle!" they all shouted out.

Can you help the Shamas place all the candles in order?

Candle Number 1... Candle Number 2...

Candle Number 3... Candle Number 4...

Candle Number 5... Candle Number 6...

Candle Number 7... and Candle Number 8.

We did it!!!! Thank you for helping the Shamas

create a Chanukah miracle.

Happy Chanukah!!!!

Let's color the Menorah Candles like a rainbow.

Candle 1 is Red.

Candle 2 is Orange.

Candle 3 is Yellow.

Candle 4 is Green.

Candle 5 is Blue.

Candle 6 is Indigo.

Candle 7 is Violet.

And Candle 8 is Red again.

Can you connect the Train Menorah and help bring color to the Chanukah candles?

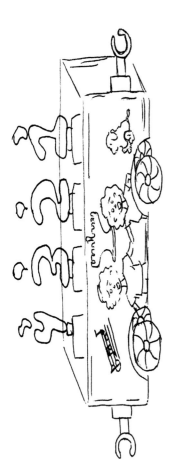

Candles are placed in the Chanukah Menorah from right to left just like when Hebrew is read. But when you light the candles, you light from left to right. By lighting left to right, the current night is first.

Made in the USA
Middletown, DE
02 December 2018